WE WENT TO VISIT
A FARM ONE DAY

Illustrated by
Jane Chapman

We went to visit a farm one day;
We saw some cows across the way,
And what do you think we heard them say?

This Walker book belongs to:

_____

_____

_____

For Abbas and Templecombe Primary School

First published 1999 by Walker Books Ltd
87 Vauxhall Walk, London SE11 5HJ

This edition published 2004

2 4 6 8 10 9 7 5 3

Text © 1999 Walker Books Ltd
Illustrations © 1999 Jane Chapman
The right of Jane Chapman to be identified as illustrator of this work
has been asserted by her in accordance with the Copyright, Designs and Patents Act 1988

This book has been typeset in Vag Roundhand and Providence Sans Bold

Printed in China

British Library Cataloguing in Publication Data:
a catalogue record for this book is available from the British Library

ISBN 978-1-84428-451-1

www.walker.co.uk

WALKER BOOKS
AND SUBSIDIARIES
LONDON · BOSTON · SYDNEY · AUCKLAND

We went to visit a farm one day;
We saw a horse across the way,
And what do you think we heard her say?

We went to visit a farm one day;
We saw some geese across the way,
And what do you think we heard them say?

We came to visit the farm today;
The animals have gone away.
There's only a big stack of hay...

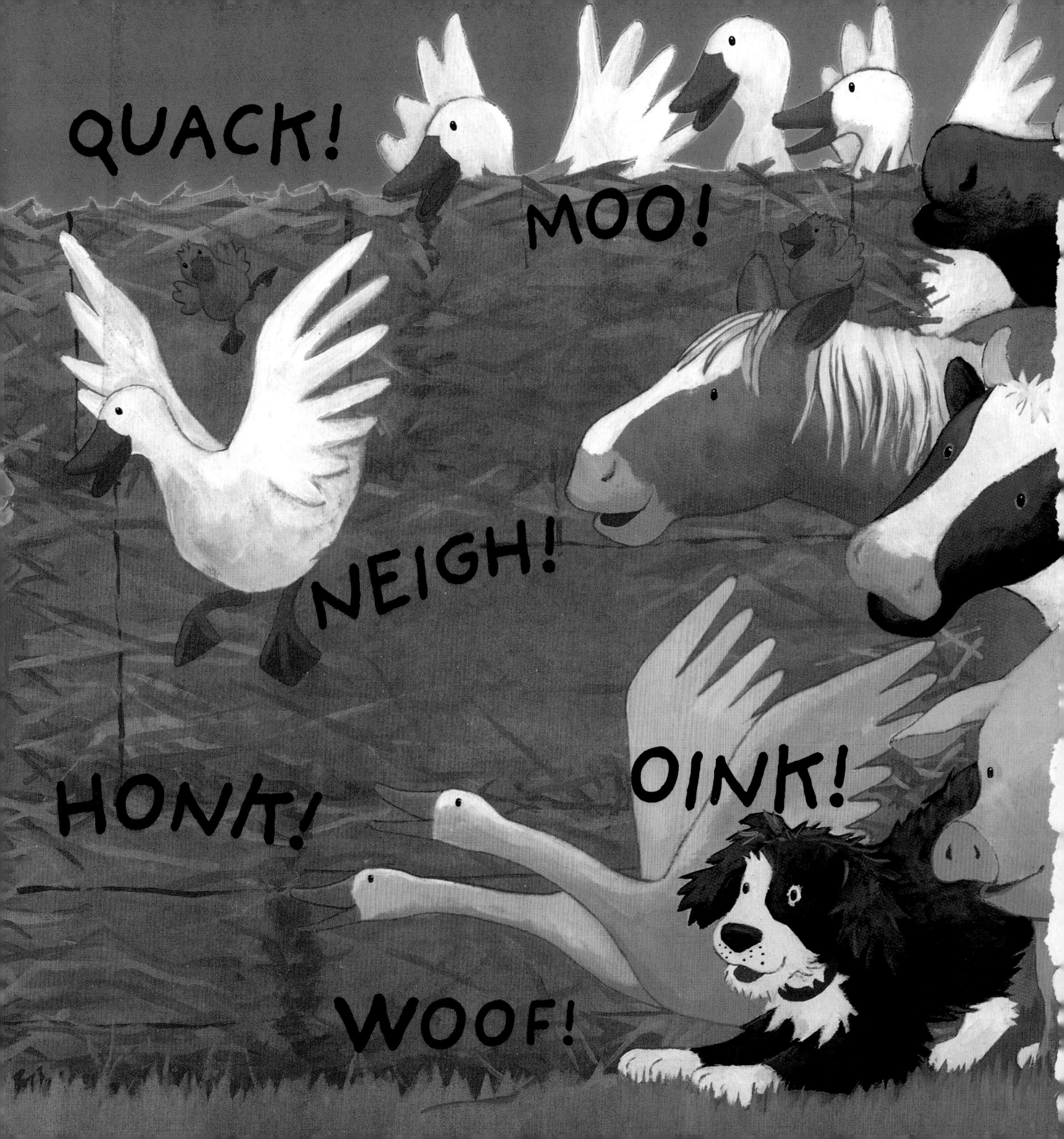
QUACK!
MOO!
NEIGH!
HONK!
OINK!
WOOF!

We went to visit a farm one day;
We saw some pigs across the way,
And what do you think we heard them say?

We went to visit a farm one day;
We saw some hens across the way,
And what do you think we heard them say?

We went to visit a farm one day;
We saw some sheep across the way,
And what do you think we heard them say?

BAA! BAA! BAA!

We went to visit a farm one day;
We saw a dog across the way,
And what do you think we heard him say?